# Thumbelina
# & The Nightingale

## Illustrated by John Patience

# Thumbelina

There was once a woman who desperately wanted a child but she could not have one. So she asked the help of an old witch. "Take this seed and plant it in a flower pot," said the witch. "Then watch what happens!"

The woman did as she was told and immediately a beautiful, tall flower grew up from the seed. The bud burst open and right in the middle of it sat a tiny girl, no bigger than your thumb. "What a pretty little child!" exclaimed the woman. "I shall call you Thumbelina."

A polished walnut shell served as Thumbelina's bed. The woman put it on her table and beside it she set a bowl of water on which floated a tulip petal. Thumbelina liked to sit on this and row herself from one side of the bowl to the other using a couple of white horse hairs as oars.

One night, as Thumbelina lay sleeping in her walnut shell, a hideous toad hopped in through a broken window pane. "She would make a nice wife for my son!" said the toad. He seized the shell and hopped back through the window and down the garden.

The toad lived with his son on the marshy bank of the stream which ran through the garden and the son was just as hideous and slimy as the father. Together they put the walnut shell out on the water on a lily pad. Then away they swam to prepare a future home for the couple in the mud patch.

When the poor little girl woke up the next morning and saw where she was she began to cry bitterly, for she was surrounded by water and couldn't reach the shore at all.

The small fishes in the stream had overheard the toad and his son talking and felt sorry for Thumbelina. They swam up to the lily pad and nibbled away at the stem until at last it broke. Then the leaf floated away down the stream, far from the loathsome toads.

A beautiful butterfly fluttered down and sat upon the leaf. Thumbelina took her sash and attached one end of it to the butterfly and the other end to the leaf. Then the butterfly helped to pull her along.

Just then a large stag beetle came flying by. Seeing the tiny girl, he took a fancy to her and, without more ado, he snatched her up and carried her into a tree. How frightened poor little Thumbelina was. But she grieved most for her friend the butterfly whom she had tied to the leaf. If he could not free himself he would starve to death!

The stag beetle seated Thumbelina on a large leaf, brought her a sweet flower to eat and proceeded to pay her compliments.

Soon the other beetles in the tree came to pay her a visit. "Oh dear, she has only two legs," said one of them. "And no feelers at all," added another. "What an ugly creature." In truth, Thumbelina was very beautiful and the stag beetle who had taken her thought so, but when he heard all the others say that she was ugly he began to believe them and lost interest in her. He decided to let her go, so he flew her down and set her on a daisy.

Despite her new-found freedom it made the little girl cry to think that she was so ugly. She could not tell it wasn't true.

Throughout the summer Thumbelina lived alone in the forest. She made a bed of grass for herself and picked flowers from which she ate the nectar and drank the morning dew.

Summer and autumn passed and winter came. Thumbelina's clothes were in rags and she was dreadfully cold. When the snow came each flake was like a shovelful to her. She wrapped herself in a dry leaf, but it was no good; she could not fight the cold.

Thumbelina wandered out of the forest and across a frozen field where she came upon a field mouse's door. The field mouse lived just under the ground in a cosy den which contained a storeroom, a kitchen and a pretty little dining room. Thumbelina begged for a grain of barley, for she had not eaten for two days and was very hungry. "You poor little thing!" said the field mouse. "Come into my warm parlour and eat with me." As they ate she became very fond of Thumbelina and said, "You are most welcome to stay with me for the winter, but you must keep my parlour tidy and tell me stories, for I do love stories."

The tiny girl accepted the mouse's kind offer and she was well looked after.

One day the mouse said, "We are about to receive a visit from my neighbour. He is better off than I am; he lives in a grand hall and wears a splendid velvet coat. If you married him your fortune would be made. He is blind so you must tell him your very best stories."

The idea of marrying the neighbour did not appeal to Thumbelina for he was a mole. Still, when he came to visit, Thumbelina sang him some songs and the mole was delighted and he fell in love with her. But he didn't say anything because he was a very shy fellow.

The mole had recently dug a long tunnel from his house to the field mouse's and the field mouse and Thumbelina could take walks there. But he warned them not to be afraid of the dead bird which lay in the tunnel. It had obviously died recently and happened to have been buried just there. "It is rather in the way," said the mole, "but it won't hurt you."

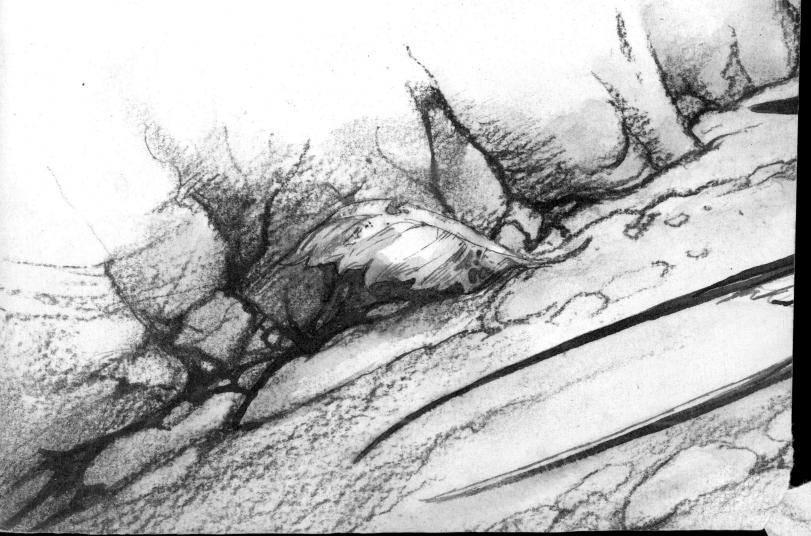

But Thumbelina recognised the bird as the one who had sung her songs in the summertime and she began to worry about him. That night she got up and covered the bird with a soft blanket.

"Farewell, beautiful bird. Farewell," she said. "And thank you for the songs you sang to me when all the trees were green." And she laid her head on its breast. She quickly sprang up again, because she heard a fluttering sound from the bird's heart. The swallow was not dead, it was just numbed with cold. Under the warm blanket the bird slowly recovered. Thumbelina looked after him all through the winter, but she told neither the mole nor the field mouse anything about him because she knew they didn't like the poor swallow.

As soon as spring arrived, Thumbelina opened up a hole above the swallow and let in the sunlight. The swallow asked her if she would like to sit on his back and fly out into the green forest. "No," said Thumbelina. "It would make the field mouse unhappy if I left her suddenly. I cannot go." So the swallow flew out into the sunlight and Thumbelina waved goodbye.

"This summer you must prepare
your trousseau," said the field mouse to
Thumbelina, for the dreary mole next door
had proposed to her. "You will need both
woollens and linen! You will need chair coverings and bed coverings when you become the mole's
wife!" Thumbelina had to spin thread and yarn and
the field mouse hired four spiders to weave both day
and night.

At last the day of the wedding arrived and the mole
came to fetch Thumbelina. She would now have to
live with him deep under the ground, never to come
out into the warm sunshine again. The poor child was
so unhappy at the prospect of saying goodbye to the
beautiful sun. She had at least had permission to see it
from the doorway of the field mouse's house.

She went there for the last time, took a few steps
out through the newly-cut stalks of wheat and kissed a
little red flower. "Farewell, little flower," she said.
"If ever you see my friend the swallow, give
him my love." At that moment she heard a
joyous "tweet" and, looking up she saw the
swallow flying above her. He swooped down and
Thumbelina told him that she was to be married
to the dreary old mole and must live
deep under the ground.

"You saved my life when I lay frozen in the dark earth," said the swallow. "Climb upon my back and I will carry you far away. The cold winter is approaching and I am going to fly away to the warmer lands." So Thumbelina climbed on the swallow's back and he flew up into the air over the forest and sea and high over the beautiful snow-covered mountains.

At last they reached the warm lands. Under the green trees by a blue sea stood the ruins of an ancient castle of white marble. Many birds had built their nests at the top of the columns. The swallow flew down with Thumbelina and set her on the petals of one of the flowers growing in the cracks of a broken column which lay on the ground. Inside the flower stood a tiny man. On his head he wore a golden crown and on his shoulders a pair of tiny wings. He was the prince of the flower spirits.

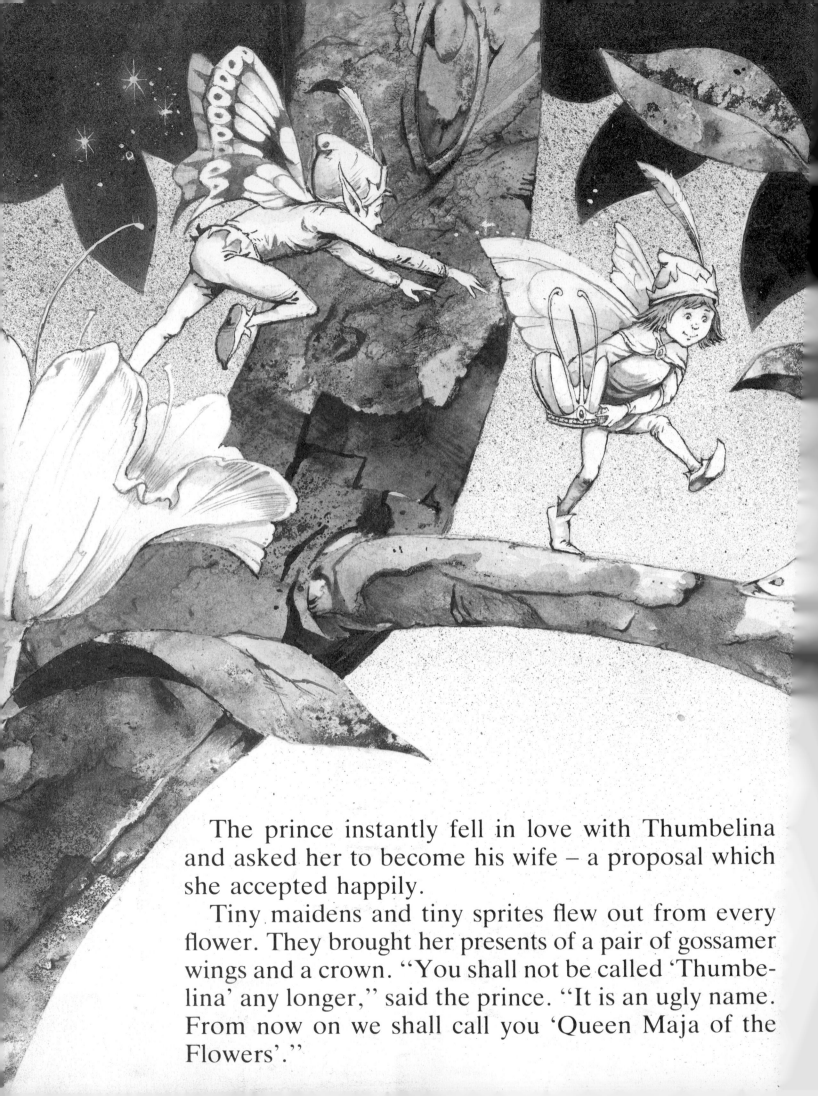

The prince instantly fell in love with Thumbelina
and asked her to become his wife – a proposal which
she accepted happily.

Tiny maidens and tiny sprites flew out from every
flower. They brought her presents of a pair of gossamer
wings and a crown. "You shall not be called 'Thumbelina' any longer," said the prince. "It is an ugly name.
From now on we shall call you 'Queen Maja of the
Flowers'."

# The Nightingale

Long ago in China there lived an emperor. His palace was the most magnificent in all the world. Close by the palace grew a forest. Here lived a nightingale who sang so sweetly that even the fishermen would stop their work to listen to its song.

Travellers came from far and wide to see the palace, but when they heard the bird singing they declared that it was the loveliest thing of all.

The emperor never left his palace and did not know about the nightingale until he read of it in a book. Then he demanded that it be brought to sing for him. So, that night the little brown bird sang in the palace for the great emperor. The nightingale's song was so sweet that tears came to the emperor's eyes and ran down his cheeks. "That was beautiful," he sobbed. "You must stay in the palace and sing for me whenever I command it."

One day a package arrived for the emperor. It was a gift of a mechanical nightingale from the emperor of Japan. It was made of gold and silver, and studded with precious stones. When it was wound up it sang. The song was just as beautiful as the real nightingale's and it could sing it over and over again without becoming tired.

The emperor declared that the real nightingale was inferior to the mechanical one and must therefore be banished.

A whole year passed by then one night, when the mechanical bird was singing, something went "clang" inside it. It was broken. All kinds of people were called in to mend it but it was completely worn out.

Not long after this the emperor fell ill and it was believed that he would die. "Oh, little golden nightingale," he sighed. "Sing to me and lighten my heart." But the mechanical bird remained silent, of course.

All at once a most beautiful song broke the silence. It was the real nightingale who had heard of the emperor's illness. He sat on a branch outside the emperor's window and sang to bring him hope. From that moment he began to recover and very soon he was completely well again.